SCREAMMATES

FIELD OF SCREAMS

BY
KIERAN FLYNN

INTERIOR ILLUSTRATIONS BY
JASON VEGA

AN
APPLE
PAPERBACK

SCHOLASTIC INC.
New York Toronto London Auckland Sydney

For Mom, Dad, and Jed

ISBN 0-590-09900-0

Produced by Daniel Weiss Associates, Inc.
33 West 17th Street, New York, NY 10011

12 11 10 9 8 7 6 5 4   8 9/9 0 1 2 3/0

Printed in the U.S.A.   40

First Scholastic printing, May 1998

CHAPTER
ONE

"Look out! Hey! Kid! Look out!"

It sounded like they were screaming at me, but I didn't know why. I stopped pedaling my bike.

"Are you talking to *me*?" I called.

"Yes!" screamed the big kid with black hair. "You! Look out!"

I looked all around, but I didn't see anything. What was he talking about?

"Heads up!" he yelled.

"What are you talking about?" I called. "There's noth—*ooompf*!"

That was when the baseball nailed me. It beaned me right in the forehead and knocked

1

me down. My bike flew in the air and landed on top of me.

Great. Just great.

I'd been riding around all day, trying to meet some of the kids in Carterville. And then, when I finally found some, I had to go and make a total fool of myself!

I'm cursed, I thought. I'm completely cursed!

Maybe I was overreacting, but you have to understand. My family just moved to Carterville, and I had no friends. This was the third time we had moved in two years because of my dad's job. Three new towns. Three new schools. And I was only eleven years old!

Do you know how hard it is to make friends when you're the new kid? Well, everywhere I went, I was *always* "the new kid." I felt like I needed a name tag on my shirt: *Hello! My name is Josh Thompson, and I'm the loser of the century!*

You want to know a great way to make new friends? Try getting beaned with a baseball and ending up facedown on the ground, chewing dirt, with a bike on your head. All the kids will think you're *really cool.*

"Are you okay?" asked one of the kids. It

sounded like a girl, but I couldn't see her. My face was still in the dirt.

"Mm-hmm," I grumbled as I pushed the bicycle away.

I turned over and saw eight kids staring down at me.

I wanted to talk, but I spit out a mouthful of dirt instead. They all started laughing.

"What a Muldoon!" said a kid wearing huge glasses.

"Yeah," a superskinny girl agreed. "*Total* Muldoon! Ha-ha!"

I didn't know what a "Muldoon" was, but it did *not* sound like a compliment.

"Leave him alone," said a short girl with blond hair. "Zack's home run just beaned him in the head. He might have brain damage or something."

She knelt down next to me.

"Hey, kid," she said, "can you hear me? Do you remember your name?"

"Yeah," I answered. "My name's Josh . . . Josh Thompson. I'm new in town."

"Yeah, no *duh*!" The big kid with black hair laughed.

They all laughed.

"Shut up, Zack!" yelled the blond girl.

She turned back to me.

"Well, my name's Amanda," she said. "And this is Zack Flannigan." She was pointing to the big kid with black hair. "He's the one who almost killed you."

She introduced the rest of the kids to me. The superskinny girl was Twiggy. The big-glasses kid was Supersonic. There was an incredibly fat kid named Turbo, another kid named Buzzcut, and twins, Timmy and Tammy.

I sat up and brushed the dirt off myself. At least Amanda was being nice to me.

"Uh . . . it's nice to meet you all," I said.

"Yeah, well, we gotta get back to our game," Zack announced. "Good luck with your head."

That was it? That was all they had to say to me? *Good luck with your head?* Oh, man! I was going to have to ask my least favorite question in the world.

"Wait a minute," I blurted. "Uhhh . . ."

I hated doing this.

"Can I play?" I asked. Lame!

They all stopped walking.

"Are you any good?" asked Zack.

"I practice every day," I said, holding up my

glove. I've learned to bring a baseball glove when I'm looking for new friends.

"Okay," Zack said. "Take center field. I'm gonna hit you a few."

"Cool!" I yelled, sounding a little too excited.

The kids giggled as I ran to center field.

"What a Muldoon," I heard Turbo mutter.

They all ran back to the plate to watch Zack hit fly balls out to me. He was obviously the big hitter of their team.

What was I getting myself into?

The truth was, even though I practiced all the time in my backyard, I wasn't good under pressure. Now I was all alone out there, trying out for these kids I didn't even know!

And it was a total nightmare.

I couldn't catch a thing!

Zack would hit the ball and I'd start dancing around center field, trying to figure out where the ball was going.

The more I danced, the more they laughed. The more they laughed, the more I tripped. And I mean *tripped*. I was toppling over left and right. I should have had a baseball cap with a giant *L* for *loser*.

And they kept saying that word over and over again—*Muldoon*!

"What a *Muldoon*!" Zack cackled.

"He really *Muldooned* that one!" sneered Supersonic.

Finally Zack stopped hitting balls out to me. They walked over to me in center, snickering all the way.

"I don't think it's gonna work out," said Zack, about to laugh in my face.

"Yeah, Muldoon," Buzzcut added. "Thanks, but *no thanks*."

The group laughed again.

"Ahhh-*chloozer*!" sneezed Twiggy. She was covering her mouth and pretending to sneeze, but I heard her say "loser."

The whole gang laughed again.

"But I can play," I said. "I was just, uh . . . *dizzy* from getting hit in the head."

"Yeah, right," said Zack.

I couldn't give up. These were the neighborhood kids. If I couldn't make friends, it was going to be a *very* lonely summer. And I couldn't take another lonely summer. No way.

"Come on," I pleaded. "Hit me a few more. I got it covered—"

"I don't think you're hearin' me, Muldoon!" Zack interrupted. "I'm saying *get off the field.* We're trying to play some real baseball here!"

"I can play real baseball!" I insisted.

"Off the field!" Zack roared, putting his face right in front of mine.

"No!" I said firmly. "Not until you give me another shot."

There was a long silence as Zack stared me down.

But then the expression on his face changed. It went from a mean stare to a crooked sort of smile.

"Okaaaay," he said, smiling and looking around to all the other kids. "Tell you what, Muldoon. Why don't you meet us for another tryout . . . *tonight.*"

"Tonight?" said Buzzcut. "What are you talk—?"

"Yeah, *tonight*!" Zack interrupted, giving Buzzcut a dirty look. He turned back to me. "Meet us tonight at Carterville Stadium."

"Zack!" yelled Amanda.

"What?" he replied.

"You can't tell him to go to—!"

"We're *all* gonna meet at Carterville

Stadium!" Zack interrupted. "Tonight at eight o'clock. Come on, guys! It'll be fun. You want to meet us, don't you, Muldoon?"

"My name's Josh," I said. "And yeah. I want to play."

"Then it's settled," Zack announced. "Eight o'clock at Carterville Stadium. Just follow this road down about a mile. You'll see the sign for the stadium. It's kind of covered by paint and vines and stuff. But it's there. Then you just have to walk a little through the woods to get to the stadium. But you'll find it. You'll *definitely* find it. See ya there."

He still had that weird smile on his face.

I started to feel a little nervous. But I had to go through with this.

"Definitely," I said, trying to look as cool as possible. "I'll be there."

They all started to walk off the field, giggling. But Amanda wasn't laughing at all. She looked scared.

"See you tonight," she said in a quavering voice. She kept looking back at me as they walked away.

"Be careful!" she added.

Careful? Careful of what?

And what was a stadium doing buried in the woods?

CHAPTER
TWO

I waited until seven-thirty to leave the house. I wasn't sure how long it would take me to find the place. Especially since Carterville was way dark.

Once I had biked away from all the houses, there were no lights anywhere on the road. The only way I could see anything was by moonlight and with this little flashlight I had on my key ring.

I followed Zack's instructions and started pedaling down the road.

The wind was picking up. It was pounding against my eardrums. And the road was getting rocky. I could barely see in front of my face.

This was a bad idea, I thought.

Why weren't there any lights coming from the stadium?

Why weren't there any lights at all? It looked like no one ever came out this way.

I was trying to use my little flashlight and pedal in the dark, but I was losing my balance. The bike started swerving and bumping over bigger and bigger rocks. Tree branches were swiping against my shoulders as I went flying by. Was I even on the road anymore?

"Hello?" I called out.

But all I could hear was the wind whistling in my ears.

I started swerving off the road. My bike was out of control!

"Hello? Is anybody—*whoa*! Whoooooaaaaa!"

Thud!

I flew off my bike and scraped across the ground.

When I looked up, I had found the sign. Or what was left of it. I shined my flashlight on it. All I could read was

CARTEV   STAD

The rest was completely covered in graffiti. There was that word again, written all over the sign: *Muldoon*, or *Muldoon Stinks!*, or *Get Out of Town, Muldoon!*

That's when I heard it.

"Uuuuuuugh."

It sounded like someone moaning from a serious illness.

"Uuuuuuugh. Uuuuuuuugh."

It wasn't loud. It was coming from far away. It was sort of floating in the wind.

"Uuuuuuugh. Uuuuuuugh."

"Hello!" I shouted. *"Hello!"*

But all I heard was wind.

"Amanda? Zack?"

Nothing. Just wind. And it was way too dark.

I wanted to leave, but I couldn't even tell which way *was* home anymore.

"Uuuuuugh. Eauuuuuugh!"

There it was again! And now it was louder! Echoing from every direction! A sick, scratchy moan, pulsing in my ears!

I had to get to the stadium. The other kids had to be there already. I definitely did *not* want to be alone anymore.

I picked myself up and started running

through the woods, calling out for the other kids, shining my little flashlight beam to try to see in front of me.

I was running through trees and bushes that kept slapping me in the face and hitting me on the arms. My flashlight didn't help. I tried to aim it at the ground so I wouldn't fall. But there were fallen branches everywhere.

Where was this place?

"Hello? You guys? Amanda?"

I couldn't see anything but trees. Just branches and leaves.

"Hey! Where are you guys? Is anybod—*oooompf*!"

Ow! I had run full speed into a huge brick wall. I fell backward onto the ground.

My head was pounding. Everything was spinning. I could barely catch my breath.

But I had found it.

It was written in huge metal letters that were shining in the moonlight. The letters were at least twenty feet above me:

CARTERVILLE STADIUM

There were no lights on at all. I shined my flashlight around.

The place was huge. And it was covered with dirt and vines and graffiti. The graffiti was just like on the sign on the road. *Muldoon Is a Loser* or *Cubs Are the Worst*!

There were even holes in the walls. The bricks were crumbling.

Carterville Stadium was totally abandoned.

And there were no kids in sight. I was alone.

"Uuuuuuugh. Ugh-huh-huuuuuuuuugh."

Oh, man! The sound again!

It was much closer now. Much louder, too. And it wasn't just moaning—it was all-out sobbing. Someone was crying. Someone inside the stadium.

That's not a kid's voice, I thought. It's a *man's* voice.

Suddenly a hand grabbed my neck!

"Aaaaaaaaaahhhh!"

CHAPTER
THREE

"Josh! Calm down!"

"Aaaaaaaaahhhhh!" I couldn't stop screaming.

"Josh! It's me. Amanda!"

I turned around to see Amanda standing there with her bike.

"You scared me to death!" I yelled.

"I'm sorry," she replied. "Do you want me to go?"

"No!" I said quickly. "No, no. I'm sorry! Don't go! Did you hear it? Did you hear *him*?"

"Hear *who*?" she asked, looking at me as if I were nuts.

"I don't know who! In there! Moaning. Crying. Someone is in there crying!"

"Wait!" Amanda said. She started to look a little scared. Her eyes got a little wider, and her hands

15

started trembling. It was like she *knew* what I was talking about.

"You heard someone crying inside?" she asked, her voice quavering.

"Yes, that's what I'm saying!" I shouted. "Didn't *you* hear it?"

"No," she said as she started to move away from the stadium. "But I think we should get out of here *right now*."

"Tell me what's going on!" I insisted. "Where have you been? Where's everybody else?"

"Josh, let's go!"

"Just answer my question!" I demanded.

"It was a joke, Josh!" she yelled back. "Okay? I'm sorry! I didn't know. Zack and the other guys weren't really gonna come. They just wanted to scare you. When I found out they weren't gonna come, I came here to find you. Now let's get out of here!"

"I can't believe it!" I cried, pounding my hand against the stadium wall. "I'm such an idiot! It's always the same. It's just another town where I'm not going to make any friends. I'm such a loser! I'm the loser of the century!"

"*Uuuuuuuugh! Uuugh-huh-huuuuuuuugh!*"

The man's voice let out a huge cry. It was the biggest and loudest sob yet.

"Aaaaaaaahhhh!" screamed Amanda.

"Did you hear *that*?" I asked.

"Yes, I heard it!" she yelped. Her legs were wobbling like crazy. "Now let's get out of here, Josh! You don't know what's going on here, but I think *I* do! Come on!"

That's when the voice spoke.

"Wait," the voice whispered.

"Aaaaaaahhhh!" Amanda screeched. "Josh, come on!"

"Pleeeeeease," the voice moaned. *"Don't go yet. Uuuugh-huuuuugh."*

The sound of footsteps started coming from inside the stadium entrance. Someone was walking toward us!

"Who's there?" I asked timidly, trying to aim my flashlight down the long dark hall leading into the stadium.

All I could see was the shadow of someone . . . or some*thing*.

It reached a hand out toward me!

"Help meeeeeeee," it moaned. *"You can help meeeeeeee!"*

"Amanda . . . ," I said, shivering.

"Yeah?" she said, frozen from shock.

"Run!"

18

CHAPTER
FOUR

We ran back through the bushes as fast as we could. Amanda was leading the way with her bike. *She* had a nice *big* flashlight.

I grabbed my own bike off the gravel and we *burned rubber.* We just pedaled like crazy until we got back to the neighborhood.

It was the first time I was happy to see my new house in Carterville.

I threw my bike down in my yard and dropped to my knees, trying to catch my breath. Amanda threw hers down, too. Neither one of us could even talk. But I had some *major* questions to ask!

"Okay!" I shouted, still panting. "What's going on here?"

"What do you mean?" Amanda asked, gasping for breath.

"*What do I mean?*" I yelped. "What do I *mean*? I mean who *was* that? *What* was that? And why is Carterville Stadium totally abandoned? *That's* what I mean!"

"Okay! Okay!" she barked, grabbing my shoulders. "Just *calm down*, okay?"

"I'll calm down when you tell me what that was!" I snapped.

"Look," she said, "I'm not sure, but I think we just saw a ghost. *The ghost of Red Muldoon.*"

"*What* is Red Muldoon?" I begged. "Will someone *please* tell me what a Muldoon is?"

"Not *what*," said Amanda. "*Who.*"

I was totally confused.

"Red Muldoon is not a thing," she continued. "He's a person."

"Well, who is he?" I asked, exasperated.

"I'm trying to tell you!" she replied.

Amanda finally caught her breath. And she started explaining.

"Red Muldoon was the pitcher for the 1927 Carterville Cubs. See, way back then, the Carterville Cubs were a great team in the minor leagues. And they made it to the championship series against the Visalia Vultures!"

"Yeah, so?" I said.

"It was a great series," she continued. "A total fight to the finish. And it all came down to one big game at Carterville Stadium.

"It was the top of the ninth, two strikes, two outs, and one man on. Muldoon was pitching to the Vultures' biggest slugger, Bugsy McGee. He only needed one more strike for the Cubs to win the championship.

"But McGee creamed it! He smacked it over the fence, and the Cubs lost the series.

"It was all Red Muldoon's fault. Everyone hated him. The whole town hated him. They just kept *booing* and *booing*. And they were *so* angry, they *never* came to another Cubs game. No one ever bought another ticket. That's why the stadium is abandoned. All because of Red Muldoon.

"He was the biggest loser this town has ever known. He was, like, the loser of the century. And to this day, a loser in Carterville is called a real *Muldoon*.

"No one knows what happened to Red Muldoon for sure. But they say that his ghost haunts Carterville Stadium. That's why no one will go near the place. And Josh . . . *I think that we just saw him*!"

"You really think it was him?" I asked, trembling.

"Yes," said Amanda, grabbing my arm. "And Josh . . . ," she whispered. There was a really serious expression on her face. "I think he was coming for *you*!"

CHAPTER
FIVE

I was way too scared to go to bed that night. Ghosts always come to you when you're in bed.

Instead I went out to the backyard and practiced catching fly balls. My dad had given me an automatic ball machine for my eleventh birthday so I could practice without him.

I caught a few, but I wasn't really concentrating. How could I? The ghost could be anywhere! What did he want? Was he really coming for me?

I was trying not to think about it. But that didn't last very long.

"*Uuuuuuuuugh.*"

The moaning! It was the same moaning I'd

heard in Carterville Stadium. But I was nowhere *near* Carterville Stadium.

"Who's there?" I called out.

"*Uuuuuuuuuugh!*"

"Where are you?" I shouted.

I was spinning around in my backyard, looking in every direction. But all I saw were trees and grass and a dark sky.

Baseballs were still flying out of the machine. They were dropping all around me.

"Hello?" I whispered.

"*Pleeeeeeeease,*" the voice moaned. "*Heeeeeelp meeeeeeee.*"

Where was it coming from?

"Go away!" I yelled. I was so scared, I could hardly speak. "G-G-G-Get out of here!"

Suddenly the voice whispered right into my ear.

"*I neeeed your heeelp.*"

I jumped back and started flailing my arms around me.

"Get away from me!" I shrieked. "I c-c-can't help you! Just go away!"

Then the whispering changed to a different sound.

A much *angrier* sound. A low kind of grumbling.

24

Oh, no, I thought. I made him angry.

The ball machine started to pick up speed. The balls were flying out faster and faster!

"C-C-C-Cut it out!" I squeaked.

But it didn't do any good. The grumbling was getting louder, and the balls were coming quicker.

Pow! Pow! Pow! Pow! Pow!

It was raining baseballs!

I was trying to dodge them. I was ducking down, leaping up, covering my head, but I was getting socked pretty hard.

Pow! Pow! Pow! Pow! Pow!

"Stop it!" I screamed. "Please! Stop it!"

But the grumbling just got louder, and the balls came harder and faster. They were pounding against my arms, my knees, my head.

And then they weren't balls anymore.

The balls turned into *bats*!

And I don't mean *baseball* bats! I mean real *live* bats! Big black *biting* bats. With big black wings!

They gathered all around me, flapping their wings, screeching, and nibbling on me. I was trying to shake them off, but there were too many. Their wings were slapping me in the face.

"Get awaaaaaay!" I pleaded.

But they were everywhere. There must have been at least fifty of them fluttering around me, shrieking and biting!

"Leave me alone!" I begged.

I had to make a run for it.

I ran as fast as I could and took a giant leap through the back door and into my house. I stumbled up the stairs into my room, locked my door, and jumped under the covers.

And then it was quiet.

For a second.

"What's your name?"

I heard the whisper right in my ear, even though I was buried under the covers! I wrapped my pillow around my head and pushed it against my ears. This isn't happening. *This isn't happening.*

"I asked you a question!"

The pillow was ripped off my head. My window flew open, and the wind came swirling in. My covers flew up against the wall, and then—

I started floating!

I tried to grab on to my bed, but it was too late. I was floating in midair with nothing to hold on to!

"Why are you doing this?" I screamed.

"*We can play it this way if you want,*" growled the voice, "*or you could just agree to help meeee.*"

"Put me down!" I cried.

"*Stubborn kid . . . waaaaaay too stubborn!*"

I started to smell something. It was penetrating my nostrils. It smelled like . . . *smoke!*

There was smoke floating up from my bed and out of the walls!

"Hey," I said. "What are you doing? W-W-What are you—?"

Fooooomp!

Fire! The walls were on fire! And so was my bed!

My body started floating lower and lower—right toward the flaming bed. I felt the heat blazing against my face, felt my skin getting hotter and hotter. He was gonna roast me!

My body started slowly spinning around and around. . . .

He wasn't going to roast me. He was going to *barbecue* me!

I started to hear the sound of sizzling.

"*You still want to play it this way? 'Cuz I'll tell you right now, kid . . . this is nothin'. You think you're scared now? I'm just getting started. So, are*" *you going to help me? Or should I show you the next level?"*

"I'll help you!" I belted. "I will definitely help you! Absolutely! Help is on the way!" I *did not* want to see the next level. "Just please make it stop! *Make it stop!*"

"Tell me your name!" he demanded.

"My name is Josh! Josh Thompson!" I said as quickly as I could. "W-W-What's yours?"

And then everything stopped.

The fire was gone. My window was closed, and I was back in bed.

And sitting across from me was this little old man in an old-fashioned baseball uniform. He was just sitting quietly in the chair next to my bed.

"The name's Red," he said. "Red Muldoon."

CHAPTER
SIX

"*You're* Red Muldoon?" I asked, looking kind of surprised.

"Yeah, that's right," he said. "You got a *problem* with that?"

"No!" I said. "It's just . . . you're a whole lot scarier when you're invisible."

"Well, if you want me to start scaring you again—!"

"No!" I screamed. "No, please, just . . . tell me what you want me to do."

Red pulled the chair closer to my bed.

"Josh," he said, looking me in the eye, "I need a baseball team."

"Huh?" I grunted.

"You heard me," he said. "I need you to help me put a team together!"

"Why?" I asked, feeling totally confused.

"Look," he said. "Do you know what happened to me back in '27? Do you know about *that game*? Awww, who am I kiddin'? Of course you know. Everyone in Carterville knows about that game! *They never forget!*"

His face started to turn bright red with anger. Maybe that's why they called him Red.

"Yeah," I said. "I know what happened. I'm sorry that—"

"Yeah, yeah, yeah, well, *don't* be sorry. I'm no loser, you understand? *I'm no loser!*"

"Yes!" I yelled. "I understand!"

"*One pitch*, Josh. One lousy pitch and the whole town hated me. Does that seem fair to you?"

"No way," I said, shaking my head as hard as I could.

"That's why my ghost is still here, Josh. I can't get over that game. All I do is sit in Carterville Stadium and think about Bugsy McGee and that *one pitch*! He slugged it so far out of the park, no one even knew where it went. He made a fool out of me! He ruined my life! He made the whole town hate me! And he's *still* rubbing my nose in it!"

32

"What do you mean?" I asked.

"*Every ten years, Josh!*" Red said. He looked as if he were going to cry or something. "Every ten years Bugsy and the Vultures come back to Carterville Stadium. They come back on the anniversary of *that game*, just to make fun of me. Just to remind me what a loser I am! And that means they're coming back tomorrow night. *The Visalia Vultures are coming back tomorrow night!*"

"They're coming *back*?" I said, in total shock.

"That's what I'm tellin' ya!" Red cried. "And this time when Bugsy and the Vultures come back . . . I want to challenge them to another game!"

Red was yelling at the top of his lungs.

"*I want another chance! I want a rematch!*"

He pounded his fist down on my desk.

"I just need a team!" he said. "My old team won't play with me anymore. They gave up on me! They think I'm a loser!"

Suddenly he jumped at me and grabbed my arm.

"That's where you come in!" he said, with foam coming out of his mouth like a big dog. "Josh . . . you've got to get a team together for me. You're my only hope!"

"Me?" I squeaked. "Why me?"

"Because I heard you tonight at the stadium,"

Red said. "I heard you yelling about having no friends. About being the 'loser of the century.' Don't you see? *We're the same, Josh!* Do you know what it's like to be alone all the time? To have everyone laughing at you?"

"Yeah," I said.

"Well, imagine feeling that way for the rest of your life. *And after your life!*"

I thought about the idea of being a loser for the rest of my life. You know what I thought? No way!

"I want to help you," I said. "But how can I help? The kids won't even talk to me. How am I gonna convince them to play a game at Carterville Stadium?"

"That's where *I* can help *you*," Red said with a sly smile. "I'll just *help* you convince them!"

"But how?" I asked him.

"How?" he repeated, letting out a little giggle. "Well, how did I get to *you*, Josh? *Spooks*, that's how. Spooks! They're the only good part of being a ghost!"

Yeah! I thought. We'd scare Zack and the others into playing. I mean, they sure didn't mind scaring *me*, sending me to Carterville Stadium all alone.

"Let's do it," I said.

It was time for a little revenge.

CHAPTER
SEVEN

"What are you doing, Muldoon?" Zack shouted. "Get off the field!"

I had walked right onto the field in the middle of their game and taken my place in center field. They all looked totally shocked.

"Are you talking to me?" I asked.

"Who do you think I'm talking to?" Zack replied. "I thought I told you yesterday. No Muldoons allowed!"

I just stared at Zack with a little smirk on my face.

"Are ya deaf, too?" he yelled. "Get *off* the *field*!"

"Zack," I said calmly, "I can't get off the field *now*. We have to *practice*."

"Practice for *what*?" he asked with a dopey expression on his face.

"For the big game," I said.

"What are you talking about?" he shouted.

"I'm talking about the big game we're all gonna play tonight . . . *at Carterville Stadium.*"

That shut them up. Everyone just stared at me as if I were totally nuts.

"Oh, yeah, *sure*," Zack said. "The big game at *Carterville Stadium.*"

Then he looked around at the other kids.

"Well," he said. "I guess it's official. The Muldoon has gone completely psycho!"

The whole gang laughed.

"I'm totally serious," I explained, walking slowly up to Zack until we were face-to-face. "We've been challenged to a game tonight at Carterville Stadium, and I accepted for us. So we'd better start practicing."

"Who challenged us to a game?" he asked. "No one's out there! Besides, I wouldn't go near that place if you paid me!"

"That's funny," I said. "You didn't seem to have a problem sending *me* out there! *All by myself!*"

"It was just a joke," he replied. "What's the big deal?"

I grabbed him by the shirt and pulled him down toward me.

"Real funny," I said. "Now why don't you go back to home plate and hit me some flies. We need to practice. We are playing tonight at Carterville Stadium."

Amanda ran over to me and whispered in my ear, "Josh! What are you doing?"

I was still holding Zack's shirt, but I turned to Amanda.

"Just go with me on this," I whispered. "Trust me."

She nodded and turned to Zack.

"Zack!" she shouted. "I think we should take the challenge! We never back down on a challenge!"

"What's the matter, Zack?" I said. "You *scared*? Do I smell something . . . *Kentucky fried*?"

Zack pushed me away hard.

"Okay, Muldoon!" he yelled. "You want me to hit you the ball? I'll hit you the ball. But I'm tellin' you right now! That ballpark is totally spooked! There is no way, and I mean *no way*, I'm going anywhere near Carterville Stadium!"

"You're gonna change your mind," I said.

"Yeah, right!" he said, giving me another push.

I turned back to Amanda quickly.

"Whatever happens," I whispered, "don't get scared, okay?"

"Scared of *what*?" she demanded.

"You'll see."

CHAPTER
EIGHT

Zack walked back to the plate and hit me a long fly. I was feeling totally confident. I lined right up with the ball and caught it. No problem.

I pulled my arm way back and threw the ball back at Zack. But the throw didn't come down. In fact, the ball started picking up speed! Now, my arm's pretty good, but it isn't *that* good!

The other kids just dropped their jaws and watched as the ball zoomed faster and faster toward Zack.

Zack grabbed his glove from the dirt. He wanted to catch my throw, which was picking up even more speed.

"I got it!" he announced.

The question was, *What* did he have?

Because it wasn't a ball anymore! It was a foot-long *knife*!

It had huge, jagged blades on both sides, and it was about to slice its way straight through Zack's mitt and right into his face!

"Zack!" I screamed. "Hit the dirt!"

Zack's face changed to a look of total terror. He finally saw the razor-sharp blade that was about to slice off his hand!

"What the—?"

"Duck!" I screamed.

"Aaaaaaaaah!" shrieked Zack as he fell on the ground, covering his head with his arms.

The kids all started to laugh at him.

"What are you laughing at?" he whimpered. "Did you see that? Did you see it?"

"Yeah." Turbo laughed. "I saw you hiding in the dirt from a *baseball*! Ha-ha! What a Muldoon! Ha-haaaa!"

"What are you talkin' about, a baseball?" screamed Zack. "That was no *baseball*! That was a—!"

Zack looked behind him and saw one little baseball sitting on the ground. There was no knife in sight.

"Nice one, Red," I whispered. "Very nice."

"You ain't seen nothing yet, kid," whispered the voice of Red Muldoon.

Next thing I knew, Zack picked himself up, dusted himself off, and grabbed his bat. He was trying to act cool, like nothing had happened. But the kids were still laughing at his sudden fear of baseballs.

"Shut up!" he commanded. "Let's just play, all right? Twins! This one's going to you!"

Zack hit a grounder out between the twins—Timmy at second, Tammy at shortstop. They both ran full speed for the ball, and they both missed it. It rolled right between them, and they ended up whamming into each other. Total collision!

But then, when they got up together . . . they really got up *together*!

Timmy and Tammy were melded into one!

They looked like a two-headed, four-legged monster! Their bodies were connected by a huge mound of flesh that ran all the way down from their necks to their waists.

The entire gang started shrieking at the top of their lungs.

I guess they *all* could see this one.

The twins were screaming into each other's faces as they waddled all around the field.

"*Aaaaaahhhhh!*" they screamed, or should I say, *it* screamed. "*Aaaaaaaahhhhh! Aaaaaaaaahhhhh!*"

"Let go of me!" screamed Timmy.

"I'm not doing anything! Let go of *me*!" Tammy begged.

They kept trying to waddle over to the other kids for help, but no one wanted to touch the disgusting, fleshy beast. They were bad enough to *look* at!

Everyone was just running in all directions, trying to escape the monster and screaming. It was total chaos.

And then suddenly the twins were separate again.

Like the whole thing hadn't happened!

"What's going on here?" asked Twiggy.

"Yeah!" yelped Buzzcut. "What's happening?"

"We're just practicing," I said with a calm smile. This made Amanda giggle.

But it made Zack *very mad*.

Zack started charging at me like a bull. He knocked me right into the dirt, sat on top of me, and started screaming in my face.

"What's going on here, Muldoon? Are *you* doing this? *Huh?*"

"Get off me!" I screamed. "I'm not doing anything!"

"You're a liar!" he yelled. "You're a lying *Muldoon!*"

Zack reached his arm back and made a fist. He was gonna pound me.

"I'm not Muldoon!" I insisted. *"That's* Muldoon," I said, pointing right behind Zack.

"Huh?" he asked. But that was all he had time to say.

A hand grabbed Zack's fist and stopped him from hitting me.

But it wasn't a regular hand.

It was a skeleton hand!

Red Muldoon was in his true form: a walking, decrepit skeleton. In a baseball cap.

Zack saw the skeleton hand holding his fist. He turned around slowly until he was looking up—*right at Red's skull!*

"Let go of him," moaned the skull, its giant teeth chomping in Zack's face.

Zack's eyes got very wide. I saw a little drool drip out of his mouth, and then—

"Aaaaaaaaaaaaaaaaahhhhhhhhh!"

Zack let out the loudest, most high-pitched screech I had ever heard.

Red grabbed Zack with his bony hands and raised him into the air. Zack just kept screaming and screaming.

"*If you want to talk to a Muldoon,*" Red growled, "*you talk to meeeeeeeee!*"

"It's *him!*" screamed Turbo. "It's *Red Muldoon! Run!*"

"Wait!" screamed Zack, still in Red's clutches. "Don't leave me here!"

But the other kids just started running as fast as they could. Except Amanda, who was hiding behind me.

Red held Zack up with one hand, and then he raised his other hand up in the air.

Whoooooosh!

Fire! He started a huge fire around the field! A giant wall of flame surrounded the diamond.

Everyone stopped dead in their tracks.

"*Not another step!*" Red demanded. "*Now, you all listen to me! I need a baseball team, and Josh here said he'd help me out! So you've got a choice. You can play with us tonight at Carterville Stadium . . . or I can turn up the heat. I can turn it waaaaaaaay up!*"

The flames burst even higher. They started closing in on us!

"*Is that what you want?*" Red's voice boomed. "*Do you want me to turn up the heat?*"

"Nooooooo!" screamed the kids.

"*Don't make a loser angry!*" Red shouted. "*You don't want to see a loser angry!*"

Red pulled Zack closer.

"*Now, are you gonna play tonight or not? What's it gonna beeeeee?*"

"We're there!" Zack squeaked, his whole body shaking. "No question, man! We're there all the way! Tonight! Carterville Stadium! You got it! *Right, guys?*"

"Oh, yeah!" they all agreed, nodding like crazy. "You can count on us!"

"Glad to hear it," said Red, dropping Zack back on the ground.

The fire disappeared.

"Well," I said. "What are we waiting for? Let's start this practice!"

CHAPTER
NINE

I couldn't believe I was back at Carterville Stadium. Just last night I'd had the biggest scare of my life there. But there I was, waiting with Amanda, back in front of the same gigantic entrance and the same broken-down walls. And it was just as dark as ever.

"Do you think they'll show?" I asked Amanda, pointing my flashlight at her face.

"Definitely," she said.

And she was right. Just a few seconds later the entire team came rustling through the trees and the bushes. Zack ran into the stadium wall just like I had. *Oooompf!*

"Ow!" he blurted, rubbing his head. He was

waving his flashlight in every direction.

They all were.

I guess we were all completely spooked because none of us knew what would happen next.

"Well . . . ," Twiggy whimpered, "we're here. *Now* what?"

"Follow me," I said, pointing down the long dark hall that led into Carterville Stadium.

It seemed like the hallway went on forever. And the walls were completely covered with angry graffiti. Our footsteps echoed loudly in the gloom.

When we finally came out into the stadium, it was pitch-black.

"Where's Muldoon?" Turbo asked, trembling.

Suddenly all the lights in Carterville Stadium popped on. The burst of light came glaring into our eyes, practically blinding us.

When I could finally see again, I looked down at the pitcher's mound and there was Red.

He looked more like the Red I'd met in my bedroom. Just a little old guy in an old baseball uniform. The others calmed down a little when they saw him looking normal.

Red let out a big smile. He was psyched to see his team had shown up for the big game.

We all headed to the mound and shook hands with him.

"So where's the other team?" asked Zack.

"They should be here any second," Red replied.

"Who are we playing?" Supersonic asked.

"Josh didn't tell you?"

"I never got around to it," I explained.

"So who is it?" Zack asked, looking a little worried.

"Who do you think?" said Red. "The Vultures, of course. We're playing the Visalia Vultures for the 1927 championship!"

"The *Vultures*?" Zack squawked. "But they're all dead!"

"Well . . . ," Red said, "they're not *exactly* dead."

I felt my stomach jump up into my throat.

"Wait a minute!" I cried. "W-W-What do you mean, *not exactly dead*?"

"See for yourself," Red said as he looked at his watch. "They should show up in about five seconds! Four . . . three . . . two . . ."

CHAPTER
TEN

Suddenly I heard the most horrible noise I've ever heard in my life. It was like a growl. And a groan. And a moan. All at the same time. And the ground on the field was starting to *rumble*.

"*Aaauuuuuurrrrrrrrrrrrruuuuuuuuuuuugh!*"

We were all starting to lose our balance.

Amanda fell down hard.

Something was trying to come out of the ground where she'd been standing.

"*Uuuuurrrrrrrrrrrrgh!*"

The soil started to bulge up, farther and farther. Something was coming out. . . .

It was a hand! It was a bright crimson hand—*with no thumb*! It was covered with black dirt and some sort of slimy ooze. Ugh! Something was digging itself out of the ground. Something nasty. *And not quite dead!*

"*Uuuuuuuuuurrrrrrrrrrrgh!*"

We all started screaming. But we couldn't move. We couldn't even stand up. The ground was shaking so hard, there was no way to balance.

The next thing to pop out of the ground was a head! It popped out right next to Amanda's face.

"*Aaaaaaaahhhhhhhh!*" she screeched.

"*Uuuuuuuuurrrrrrrrr!*" it yelled.

The head only had one little pink eyeball left. And no remaining teeth. Just a pair of brown, slimy gums. And they were drooling even *more* slime. It used its sliminess to slide the rest of itself out of the ground.

And there it stood. Part skeleton, part man, part brown-and-crimson oozing crud.

This was one of the 1927 Visalia Vultures!

Vultures started digging themselves up all over the field. You couldn't tell *where* a hand or a head was going to pop up next. Some of them didn't even have hands—*or* heads!

"Make them stop!" cried Twiggy.

I don't know why she thought any of us could make them stop.

They just kept coming. Some of them were all bone. Some of them still had skin left. *All* of them were covered in brown slime. And all of them had some raggedy part of their old uniform still on.

"*Muldoooooon!*" growled the largest of the Vulture zombies, walking slowly toward Red.

This one was *huge*. He still had a crust of skin covering his body, but you could see his giant skeleton jutting out under what was left of his outer layer.

I had no doubt in my mind. This was the Vultures' biggest slugger.

This was Bugsy McGee!

McGee walked right up to Red on the mound and looked down at him.

"Well, if it isn't the world's biggest loser," growled McGee.

"My losing days are over!" yelled Red.

"Ha-ha! Your losing days will *never* be over, Muldoon!" Bugsy cackled.

"Well, I got me a team right here!" Red pointed to all of us sprawled out on the field, shivering with fear.

Bugsy McGee looked down at us and started

laughing. Worms were slithering out of the corners of his mouth. "What are you talking about?" he asked.

"I'm talkin' about a rematch!" Red declared. "I'm no loser! And I'm sick and tired of you and your half-eaten teammates messing with me. I'm talkin' about nine innings. Your team versus my team. What do you think about that?"

Bugsy belted out another worm-spitting laugh.

"You want *us* to play a game against you and these *scrubs*?"

"That's right!" Red announced proudly.

Suddenly Turbo spoke up.

"Uhhhh . . . excuse me," he said, still lying on the ground, "but . . . we really can't play right now. . . . We really . . . *have to get going*!"

He darted up and started running for the exit. The other kids jumped up and started running, too.

"Now hold on just a second!" growled Bugsy McGee, signaling to his teammates. The Vulture zombies grabbed hold of the kids and held them captive.

"*Aaaaaaaahh!*" screamed Buzzcut.

The Vulture holding him slapped a slimy, worm-covered hand right over Buzzcut's mouth to shut him up.

"Maybe this isn't such a bad idea," Bugsy said. "Tell ya what, Muldoon. We'll play you again. You know how I love to watch you lose! But when we win . . . *you've* gotta give *me* somethin'!"

"What do you want to play for?" asked Red.

"Well, as you can see," said Bugsy, pulling a worm from between his teeth, "my team's not looking so good. They're not in the best shape. Heck, some of 'em don't have any arms or heads! We need some fresh blood. We need some fresh *flesh*. How about these two?"

Bugsy dug his bony hand into my neck and lifted me up into the air. Then he picked up Zack with his other hand.

"No way!" screamed Zack, flailing around and completely bug-eyed.

"Let go of me!" I yelped, chills running up my spine.

"If we win," Bugsy shouted, "these two are coming back with me!"

"Noooooooo!" screamed Amanda.

"Forget it, Red!" I screamed.

Bugsy McGee pulled me right up to his rotting face. I could smell thirty years of rotting flesh on his breath. Worms were crawling all over his face.

"If you don't want to play, you don't have to!" he said. "I can just take you both with me right now. You're gonna love it underground! Ha-haaaa!"

Great. If we lost, McGee was going to take Zack and me with him. If we didn't play, he was *still* going to take Zack and me with him. That left us with only one choice.

"Red, let's play!" I screamed. "Let's play ball right now! Right *now*!"

"We *have* to do this!" Zack shouted. "I'm not ready to be a zombie! I'm just a kid!"

"All right, we'll play!" screamed Amanda. "Just let them go!"

"Let *us* go, too!" Twiggy begged.

"You heard 'em!" said Red. "We're ready to play! Now let go of my teammates!"

Bugsy dropped Zack and me to the ground. The Vultures let go of the rest of our team.

McGee let out one more huge laugh.

"This is gonna be fun," he growled. *"Play ball!"*

CHAPTER
ELEVEN

The first four innings were totally scoreless. It was all pitching. Red was playing with real fire. He was striking them out one after the other. And the Vultures' pitcher was blanking us, too. He only had one arm— but he was throwing some real heat with it!

It wasn't until the bottom of the fifth that things got *ugly*. Red had gotten two outs, but then Bugsy McGee stepped up to the plate.

Red turned kind of white. He looked a little older. He kept wiping his forehead, taking off his cap, and licking his fingers.

"You look a little nervous, Red," Bugsy taunted. "Tell you what. I won't hit it out of the park. I'll just hit it into the stands! *Ha-haaaa!*"

Red couldn't even say anything back. He just took a big gulp.

He reached back and threw his pitch. It looked weak. It looked very weak.

Crack!

Bugsy clobbered it!

He sent that thing back into the woods somewhere!

"*Woo-hoo!*" Bugsy shouted. "*Ha-haaaa!* I guess I lied! Guess I don't know my own strength, hey, Red?"

He dropped the bat and starting trotting around the bases. Little bits of slime were flying off him with every bounce of his gigantic skeleton.

My teammates moved as far from the baselines as they could. They didn't want his rotting body anywhere near them.

"Just like old times, don't ya think, Red?"

Bugsy rounded second and continued to gloat.

"Hey, Red, why don't you just call it quits? You're making losers out of all these kids!" Then he turned to Zack and me. "You boys are gonna love zombie life! *Wooooo!*"

My heart was beating way too fast. And my stomach was killing me. We were going to lose, just like Bugsy said. Just like I always do! Just like Red always does!

My life was finished!

I looked over at Red. His head was drooping.

"Come on, Red!" Zack urged. "You can do it! Just get us out of this inning! You can do it!"

"Yeah!" I agreed. "Just one more out! Smoke 'em, Red!"

No one had rooted for Red Muldoon in seventy years. He picked up his head and started to look a little stronger.

"You're right," Red said. "I ain't a goner yet, you Vultures! Who's up? I'm gonna smoke him!"

"Yeah!" I screamed.

The next Vulture came up to bat and took his stance. "Hee-hee-hee-hee-hee," he cackled. His skeleton teeth chattered in his skull.

"Oh, you think something's funny, do ya?" Red shouted. "Well, try this one on for size!"

Red kicked up his foot, cocked back his arm, and whipped the ball right into the zone.

And that ball was on fire.

I mean the ball was *really* on fire!

The Vulture's eyes opened wide, and his jaw dropped to the ground. It actually fell off his face and onto the ground!

Red's pitch came down the pike like a rocket, and the Vulture took a swing at it. But the ball burned a hole right through his bat—and set it on fire!

The flames ran down the bat and lit the Vulture's whole left arm on fire.

His arm dropped right onto home plate. It sat there, burning like a little campfire, right next to his bottom jaw.

"Strike one!"

The Vulture looked down at his lost arm and then up at Red. Red gave him a little smile.

"That's my fireball," he explained. "Now check out my lightning ball."

The Vulture looked very angry. He got a new bat from the dugout, then returned to home plate. He leaned into a low, determined stance, holding the bat with his remaining arm. "Urrrrrrrrrrgh!" he growled.

Red kicked out his leg and whipped another pitch. But it was moving way too slowly for a lightning ball. Red had messed up!

The Vulture cocked his bat way back. He was going to pound it!

But then . . . just as the ball was about to reach the plate . . . there was a sound. The sound of thunder. The sky turned even blacker.

The Vulture looked up at the sky. And just as the ball reached the plate . . .

Crack-booooom!

A huge lightning bolt came crashing down and zapped the Vulture's batting arm off! And the slow ball floated right over the plate.

"Strike two!"

The armless batter just stood there with smoke coming out of his arm sockets. It was a sorry sight. But he was still yapping.

"Uuuuuuuuurgh!" he growled.

Red held the ball out in front of him.

"And *this*," said Red, "is just a baseball."

Red tossed the ball in like he was playing catch. The Vulture had no arms. There wasn't much he could do. He just growled at the ball as it glided by him.

"Strike three! You're out of there!"

"Beautiful, Red!" I said. "Just beautiful!"

Red smiled back at me.

"That's what I call pitching!" shouted Zack.

Red took a little bow, and we all ran back to the dugout.

The score was one to nothing. We'd made it through another Vulture at-bat. But how were we ever going to score on these guys?

CHAPTER
TWELVE

We couldn't score. No matter what we did, we couldn't get a single hit. The Vultures had an answer for anything we tried.

Zack almost got a hit in the seventh. He hit one hard to left center. But the Vultures' left fielder actually threw up his right hand to catch it.

He pulled off his right hand, tossed it into the air, caught the ball bare-handed, and then caught his own hand!

It was disgusting.

It was depressing.

We went all the way to the top of the ninth, and we still hadn't scored. It was still one to nothing, and this inning was our last shot.

Twiggy was the first one up. We were rooting her on big time, but what was the use? She always had the same response:

"Aaaaaaaahhhhhh!"

Twiggy couldn't stop screaming. Not since the Vultures had shown up. I didn't think she was ever going to be the same after this game.

"Come on, Twiggy! Concentrate!" yelled Supersonic.

"Yeah!" agreed Timmy. "Just stop screaming!"

Twiggy tried to stop screaming and collect herself. She checked her footing at the plate. Checked her bat. Took a few practice swings and set up.

Then she looked down at the Vulture catcher.

"Aaaaaahhhhhhh!" she screamed.

The first pitch sailed right past her.

"Strike one!"

"Twiggy!" I said. "You've got to calm down! We've got to score! Do you understand? We have to score! Just don't look at them, okay?"

She nodded and tried to set up again.

"Don't look at them," she mumbled to herself. "Don't look at them."

So she closed her eyes!

Another pitch flew right by her.

"Strike two!"

"Twiggy!" I screamed. "Open your eyes!"

"No, no, no, no, noooooo!" she mumbled in terror.

"Twig!" shouted Zack. "If you don't open your eyes right now, I swear I'm gonna take you to zombie land with us! Open 'em!"

Twiggy's eyes popped open. The Vultures' pitcher was going into his motion. "Uuuuuurgh!" he grunted as he released the ball.

Twiggy just stood there, completely frozen. She never even moved. She didn't swing the bat.

"Strike three! You're out!"

Our whole team let out a huge moan.

"Someone get her back into the dugout," said Red.

Timmy and Tammy walked her back to the dugout, where she sat in the corner, shivering.

"We're doomed!" I moaned.

"Shut up!" Zack answered.

Amanda was up next, and I was on deck.

"Come on, Amanda!" I shouted. She was my only hope. If she could tie it, then at least it wouldn't all be in my hands.

Amanda stepped up to the plate, looking totally intense. She was definitely ready.

The one-armed pitcher smoked two pitches by her. But she didn't let it get to her. She wasn't giving up.

On the third pitch Amanda made contact. She hit a quick grounder that was going through the hole between second and third. No one was covering that spot.

"Yes!" I screamed.

Until something popped out from underground.

A baseball glove shot right out of the dirt and fielded the ball. Then the zombie shimmied halfway out of the ground and flipped the ball to first.

"Noooooo!" I exclaimed. But it was too late.

Amanda was tagged out.

That was it. There were already two outs in our last at-bat. Zack and I were only one out away from an early grave. And I was up next!

CHAPTER
THIRTEEN

I sat at the end of the dugout, freaking out. I hadn't been able to get my bat anywhere near the ball all night. What was I going to do now? Amanda came over to me.

"Don't panic, Josh," she insisted. "We're going to win this. Just don't be scared."

"How can I not be scared?" I asked. "If we lose this game, I'm totally doomed! I won't just be a loser! I'll be a *goner*!"

Suddenly Zack was in my face.

"Listen up, Muldoon!" he shouted. "I'm not going underground with these sickos. No way, no how! So we gotta work together!"

"What are you talking about?" I said. "I can't get a hit off this guy!"

"You don't need to get a hit, Muldoon. Just *make contact*, you understand? If you can bunt that ball, and if you can run it out, I will bring us home, you got it?"

"Yeah," I said. "I got it."

I was *doomed*.

I walked up to the plate and looked into the eyes of the one-armed pitcher. I don't even know how he was standing—his legs were just bones.

Just throw me a low one. That's all I need. Just one, nice and low.

I took a few practice swings, took my stance, and cocked my bat back.

The pitcher let out a little growl and threw his pitch.

Whooosh!

I could actually feel a draft from the pitch, it went by so fast.

"Strike one!"

Don't panic, I told myself. Just make contact. That's all you need to do.

The pitcher grunted and threw his next pitch.

But this one was a little slower.

Just make contact. That's all you need to do.

I placed my bat out for the bunt, and—

I made contact! Right down the third-base line!

"Run!" Zack screamed. "Run, you Muldoon!"

I took off running.

"Go, Josh! Goooo!" Amanda was screaming.

I was running as fast as I could, but something weird was starting to happen. The first-base line was starting to sink!

It was as if I were running in quicksand. It kept dropping down and down!

"Keep going, Josh!" Amanda was calling.

But my feet were getting stuck in the ground!

I heard the voice of Bugsy McGee in my ear: *"Welcome down underground, Muldoooon. Ha-haaaa!"*

I was sinking down farther and farther!

The third baseman snagged the ball and whipped it like a rocket toward first.

"Jump, Muldoon!" Zack screamed. "Juuump!"

I kicked up my feet and made a flying leap out of the ditch. I slapped my foot on first base right before the Vulture caught the ball.

"Safe!"

I did it! I was safe on first! Yesssss!

"*Yeeeeaaah!*" my team cheered.

"Zack!" I called. "I'm here, man! Now bring it home!"

Zack was already heading to the plate. He had a crazed look in his eye.

He walked up to the plate and took his stance. No practice swing, no batting his cleats. Nothing. Just a stance.

"Come on, zombie boy!" he teased. "Let's go, bones! Right down the middle! I ain't goin' underground! I'm goin' *downtown*!"

The Vultures' pitcher took Zack's dare and threw one right down the middle. Only it wasn't a ball—it was a foot-long knife!

"I'm not fallin' for *that* one again!" Zack boasted.

He pulled back, and he ripped the knife! He actually hit the knife!

Clanggg!

And—*boom!*—the knife was a ball again! It flew out over the field . . . and over the fence!

"*Yeeeeeeahhh!*" screamed the team.

"*Uuuuuuurrrrrrrrgh!*" growled the Vultures.

We had taken the lead!

Now we just had to keep it.

CHAPTER
FOURTEEN

Red stayed strong most of the way through the bottom of the ninth. We still had the 2–1 lead, and Red already had two outs.

But his arm was starting to get tired. I could tell. He was barely tossing the ball in, and he was missing the plate.

And then he gave up a base hit!

The Vulture player got to first, and he started trying to freak out Twiggy. Which was very easy. All he had to do was stand next to her, gargling his slime, and Twiggy would start screaming.

Meanwhile, Bugsy McGee stepped to the plate. Red could hardly throw heat anymore. He managed to get McGee to foul off two pitches, but Red was definitely looking *weak*.

Then I realized . . .

We had come to the exact same situation as the game in 1927!

Everything was identical!

Two strikes. Two outs. One man on.

Bugsy McGee was the winning run at the plate. And Red Muldoon was pitching.

Oh, no. This looked *very bad*!

"Remember, Muldoon?" growled Bugsy McGee. "It all came down to this one right heeeere! Ha-haaaa! So let's just get it over with, loser! Toss it in there!"

Red kept wiping his hands all over his uniform and wiping off his forehead. He must have been sweating like a pig.

"Come on, Red!" I cheered. "Burn it in there!"

"Yeah, come on, Red!" screamed the rest of the team. "No batter!"

Red took a step back . . . and he let it rip right down the middle.

Crack!

Bugsy was all over it!

The ball was going back, back . . .

It was coming straight toward me in center!

"Mine! Mine!" I shouted.

And I took off for the center field fence. The ball was carrying fast. I put on all the speed I had.

"Come on, Josh!" I heard Amanda screeching.

"Get that ball!" Zack hollered. "*Get that baaaall!*"

"*Pleeeeeeease!*" screamed Red.

I was running and running. Trying to keep my eye on the ball. But it just kept going. And suddenly—

I started to hear booing.

"*Booooooo! Booooooo!*"

It was rumbling and echoing from all around Carterville Stadium.

"*Boooooo! Booooooooo!*"

I looked out to the stands—and gasped. The stadium was filled with the most horrifying ghosts and ghouls you could ever imagine.

Hideous, disgusting creatures in every single seat!

And they were all laughing at me!

Laughing, hissing, booing, moaning!

"*What a Muldooooooooon!*" they moaned. "*Look at him! Ah-ha-ha- ha-haaaa!*"

My feet weren't running on the field anymore. I was on something strange . . . not solid. . . .

Snakes!

Snakes had covered the field!

There were all different kinds of snakes, slithering in and out of a mass of snakes, on top of one another, under one another! Everywhere!

They were flicking their tongues and snapping their fangs with every step I took!

Eye on the ball, Josh! Keep your eye on the ball!

My eyes darted back to the ball.

And the *ball* had its eyes on *me*! It had huge, red, demon eyeballs! And razor-sharp teeth!

And it was coming at me, fast!

"You'll never catch me, Muldooooon!" it snarled.

It was heading over the fence!

I leaped off the snake-infested field into the air. Reached my glove to the top of the fence. Stretched for all I was worth . . .

The ball sank its fangs right through my glove, right through the flesh of my hand.

I fell into the swarm of snakes! And then—

The booing stopped.

And the snakes were gone.

And there wasn't a sound in Carterville Stadium.

I looked down into my glove . . . and there was the ball.

I got it.

"*I got it!*" I declared at the top of my lungs, holding the ball high above my head.

"He got it!" Red agreed cheerfully.

"*Yeeeeeeeaaaaaaaahhhh!*" screamed the team.

But it was more than just my team.

I looked up into the stands.

They were *all* cheering.

And they weren't ghosts or ghouls anymore. They were just regular people. In old-fashioned clothes.

It must have been the same crowd from 1927!

The entire stadium was screaming and hooting! Celebrating!

My teammates came running toward me. They raised me up on their shoulders and paraded me around the infield.

I looked over at the mound, and there stood Red.

Only he wasn't an old man anymore. He was

a young guy in a bright, clean uniform with a giant grin on his face.

The Vultures were moaning and growling, but you could barely hear them. They just walked over to their holes, with their heads hanging low, and climbed back down underground—where they belonged!

Young Red walked over to us all.

"Thank you," he told us. "You've changed everything. You've made it right." He leaned down to me and put out his hand. "I knew we could do it, Josh," he said. "I knew it."

I shook his hand and grinned.

"It's your stadium now," he told me.

He turned around and walked toward the stadium exit.

He threw up his cap . . . and disappeared.

The entire crowd disappeared with him.

"That catch was awesome!" screamed Amanda, hitting me on the arm.

"Thanks," I said.

Zack walked up to me and slapped me on the back.

"That was a great catch, Muld—I mean, *Josh*. That was a great catch, Josh."

"Thanks," I said.

"Hey," Zack said. "Let's all meet here tomorrow for a game!"

"Definitely!" the gang agreed.

"You're gonna be there, right, Josh?" Zack asked.

"Definitely," I said.

We had all started to leave the stadium when I heard a voice whisper in my ear: *"I'm looking forward to our rematch, Thompson!"*

It was the voice of Bugsy McGee!

"Bugsy McGee is no loser!" he whispered. *"So don't think ya can get rid of me so easy!"*

"Did anyone hear that?" I cried.

"Hear what?" asked Amanda.

"Oh . . . nothing," I said. "Never mind."

"Ha-haaaa!" laughed the scratchy voice of Bugsy McGee. *"See ya in ten yeeeeeears!"*